Samuel French Acting 1

Lettie

by Boo Killebrew

FOR PRODUCTION ENQUIRIES

UNITED STATES AND CANADA
info@concordtheatricals.com
1-866-979-0447

UNITED KINGDOM AND EUROPE
licensing@concordtheatricals.co.uk
020-7054-7200

Each title is subject to availability from Concord Theatricals Corp.,
depending upon country of performance. Please be aware that
LETTIE may not be licensed by Concord Theatricals Corp. in your
territory. Professional and amateur producers should contact the
nearest Concord Theatricals Corp. office or licensing partner to verify
availability.

MUSIC USE NOTE

IMPORTANT BILLING AND CREDIT REQUIREMENTS

LETTIE was originally commissioned and produced by Victory Gardens Theater (Chay Yew, Artistic Director) in Chicago, Illinois from April 6, 2018 – May 6, 2018. The production was directed by Chay Yew, with set design by Andrew Boyce, costume design by Melissa Ng, lighting design by Lee Fiskness, and composition and sound design by Mikhail Fiksail. The production stage manager was Cassie Calderone. The cast was as follows:

LETTIE . . . . Caroline Neff
MINNY . . . . Charin Alvarez
CARLA . . . . Kirsten Fitzgerald
FRANK . . . . Ryan Kitley
RIVER . . . . Matt Farabee
LAYLA. . . . . Krystal Ortiz

CHARACTERS

LETTIE – female, mid-to-late thirties, white
MINNY – female, forties, not white
CARLA – female, forties, white
FRANK – male, forties, white
RIVER – male, seventeen, white
LAYLA – female, fourteen, Mexican-American

SETTING

Chicago and then Wisconsin

TIME

The Present

Scene One

> (**LETTIE** *and* **CARLA** *in the common room at*
> *Spring House.*)

CARLA. This is great.
    Don't you think?
    It's nice.

LETTIE. It's okay.

CARLA. Can I see your room?

LETTIE. We can't have visitors in the rooms. Just here.

CARLA. Oh. Okay, then. Well, this room here is very – I like it.
    ...
    And you have a job? Yeah? They put you –

LETTIE. It's not a job. It's a training program.
    Then a job'll come out of it.

CARLA. A welding job.
    Right?

LETTIE. I guess. Yeah.
    I don't know. We'll see.

CARLA. You know how to weld?

LETTIE. No. It's a training program.
    They'll teach me / how to –

CARLA. So you'll learn? They'll teach you / everything you –

LETTIE. In the program. Yeah.

CARLA. Oh.

> (*Reaches into her shopping bag.*)

    I got you a Brita.
    Had they come out with these?
    Before you went – have you seen these?

LETTIE. Yeah.

CARLA. Well, it filters tap water. So you can fill it up from the faucet –

CARLA.	**LETTIE.**
– And then put it in the fridge and then when you have it, it's like you're drinking bottled water. It's good. You have to change the filter every –	I don't have a sink –

LETTIE. You didn't want to bring them with you? Today?

CARLA. I don't want to rush anything.

LETTIE. I'd like to see them.

CARLA. ...

LETTIE. I want to see them soon.

CARLA. Let's just give it a minute.

LETTIE. It's...

I haven't seen them in three years. They haven't seen me, you know, in normal clothes – as a normal person – in seven. I really want them to see me, to see me now and just –

CARLA. This needs to be a gradual transition. We agreed that it should be –

LETTIE. I know what we agreed to. I'm just...

I just want to hug them. I just want to see them. That's all. Then we can go from there. I'm not asking for much here, Carlz.

CARLA. I want to let them decide.

LETTIE. Decide what?

CARLA. When.

LETTIE. Oh.

CARLA. I thought...

We could wait.

Until they're ready.

LETTIE. It doesn't have to be –

CARLA. Don't you think that's fair?

To let them decide?

LETTIE. I'm saying it doesn't have to be a big...
   You could just bring them by.

LETTIE.	**CARLA**.
I um...	Lettie.

I would really like to see
   them.

> *(Beat.)*

CARLA. I'll talk to them tonight.
   We can figure out a time.
   I'll run it by Frank –

LETTIE. Run what by Frank?

CARLA. A possible time.
   For you to come over. Have dinner.
   You can see them, see Frank, it'll be nice.

LETTIE. I'm saying it doesn't have to be some dinner.
   It doesn't have to be a big deal.
   I just want to –

CARLA. It is a big deal. For them it is a big deal.

LETTIE. I meant, like –

CARLA. We'll figure out a time.

> *(She holds up a shopping bag.)*

   I brought you some sheets, a comforter –

LETTIE. They give you that stuff / here –

CARLA. They're old and I've been meaning to get rid of
   them but it's nice to not just throw them away, when
   they're fine.
   It's River's old –
   Well, he's outgrown them.

> (**LETTIE** *opens the bag and pulls out timeworn*
> Star Wars *sheets. Then, a pillowcase.)*

   Do you – sorry.
   Do you have a pillow?

Scene Two

> (**LETTIE** *sits at a lunch table, studying a math textbook.* **MINNY** *walks in, brown lunch bag in hand.* **MINNY** *sits at another table, takes out a PB&J, a can of Mountain Dew, and chips. She eats.*)
>
> (*Quiet.*)

MINNY. You bring lunch?

> (**LETTIE** *doesn't look up from her book.*)

You eat?

Hey.

> (**LETTIE** *finally looks up.*)

You eat lunch?

LETTIE. Yeah.

> (*She goes back to her book,* **MINNY** *crunches another chip.*)

MINNY. (*Re: the textbook.*) Shit's easy, right?

LETTIE. ...

MINNY. I'm glad I'm done with the workbook shit. I'm finally doing it, you know, the actual work. Those workbooks are stupid.

LETTIE. ...

MINNY. You at Spring House?

LETTIE. (*Looks up from the book.*) How'd you know that?

MINNY. Heard you telling the lady.

LETTIE. Yeah.

MINNY. They do yoga and shit over there?

LETTIE. ...

MINNY. You don't do yoga?

LETTIE. ...

MINNY. I thought all white girls did yoga.

LETTIE. ...

MINNY. How is it? Spring House? I heard that place was shitty.

LETTIE. Yeah.

MINNY. There are some places that are really good. You try to get into a different place?

LETTIE. Yeah. But, take what you can get, right?

MINNY. I'm just saying you can get something better, probably.

You're white.

They give you guys better stuff.

LETTIE. Uh. Okay.

MINNY. When I was doing those workbooks, I was like, "I don't need to be doing this shit. I got my GED.

These are workbooks for a fifth-grader."

LETTIE. Yeah.

MINNY. Better than being a janitor, though. When I got out, I was like, "I'll do whatever but I ain't gonna be a janitor."

LETTIE. Right.

MINNY. The week I got out, my cousin got me a job being like a home care aide for this old lady.

That was good, I liked that.

We got along, me and that old lady.

LETTIE. So. Why aren't you doing that?

MINNY. Her kid found out that I had a felony.

I don't know how, but he did and he got rid of me.

And then I was like, "That's okay. I'll train and get a license to do that job for real and get another job." But then I found out I can't get no license because of that little box, you know?

LETTIE. Yeah.

MINNY. You know I tried to get a job at McDonald's?

They say they don't care about that little box, but they do.

Then my P.O. told me about this welding shit and I was like, "I don't know how to do that."

And he was like, "They teach you."

And I was like, "Is this like a dangerous situation? Is it gonna burn my shit up on the factory floor or something? Or like mutate my insides without me knowing it or some shit?"

And he was like, "No. But it's pretty much all men. No women really do it."

And I was like, "That's cool. I been around nothing but women for the past twenty years. Let's get some Y chromosomes up in my environment."

Then I came here.

It's all right.

I'm Minny.

LETTIE. Lettie.

MINNY. Lettie? That short for something?

LETTIE. No.

MINNY. Does it mean something?

LETTIE. Yeah.

MINNY. So?

LETTIE. What?

MINNY. What does it mean?

LETTIE. I don't know.

    (Beat.)

MINNY. So much better when you're working with the machines and shit.

You ain't gonna learn to do it by doing them fucking workbooks.

LETTIE. Twenty years?

MINNY. What?

LETTIE. That how long you were in?

MINNY. Yep.

In and out.

But about that, yep.

LETTIE. Logan.

Seven years.

MINNY. No shit! I was at Logan from '01 to '07.
   They had that nasty ass pudding.

LETTIE. That shit was nasty! Yes!

MINNY. But you ate it, right?

LETTIE. Yeah, but that shit tasted like cheap turkey.

MINNY. Yeah, like Spam or some shit!

LETTIE. Hell yeah it did.

MINNY. Went to MCC after Logan, though.
   That place sucked even more.

LETTIE. How long you been out?

MINNY. Six months.
   You?

LETTIE. Two weeks.

MINNY. Wow.
   Well. Welcome, I guess.

LETTIE. You got a place?

MINNY. Nah. My cousin got an extra room, so I'm staying
   there for now. But it's close, only forty-five minutes to
   get here. One bus.

LETTIE. Shit. It takes me two hours. Three buses.
   But I'm gonna find my own place soon, Spring House is
   just for now, you know.

MINNY. You like this program so far?

LETTIE. Yeah, it's fine. I mean, I just started.

MINNY. What you wanna do?

LETTIE. Like, for a job?

MINNY. No, like. Now that you're out.
   In the world, you know?

LETTIE. A lot of things.

MINNY. Like what?

LETTIE. Be with my kids, you know.
   That's the first thing.

MINNY. Oh yeah?
   You got kids?

LETTIE. Two.

Yeah.

MINNY. Who got 'em?

LETTIE. My sister.

MINNY. When you get 'em back?

LETTIE. Soon.

MINNY. So. That's it then.

LETTIE. Huh?

MINNY. You wanna be a mom.

LETTIE. I am a mom.

MINNY. But like –

LETTIE. But like a good one.

Yeah.

MINNY. Yeah. All right then.

(She raises her Mountain Dew like a toast.)

Good luck to ya.

Scene Three

> (**CARLA** *holds two shopping bags full of old clothes.*)

CARLA. Clothes for work.

LETTIE. You don't gotta keep –

CARLA. It's no problem. They're old, I don't wear them / anymore.

LETTIE. I don't need you to keep –

CARLA. You gotta have something to wear for work –

CARLA.	**LETTIE.**
To look professional.	It's a training program.

> (**CARLA** *pulls out a cardigan, some sensible pumps.*)

CARLA. Work clothes –

LETTIE. Carlz, I can't wear that shit.

CARLA. I don't wear these anymore –

LETTIE. It's a training program.

CARLA. But you want to look –

LETTIE. For welding.

> (**CARLA** *looks down at the cardigan and heels.*)

CARLA. So.
　　Jeans?

LETTIE. I got jeans.
　　I got it.

LETTIE.	**CARLA.**
You don't have to –	I'm trying to help.

> *(Quiet.)*

LETTIE. You talk to them?

CARLA. ...

LETTIE. You talk to Frank?
　　Carla?

CARLA. What?

LETTIE. Did you talk to them?

About seeing me?

About me coming over?

CARLA. I thought you didn't want to do all that –

LETTIE. You didn't.

CARLA. You told me you didn't want –

LETTIE. Carla.

CARLA. What? That's what you said. You didn't want –

LETTIE. Some fucking sit-down family dinner bullshit!

I just wanna fucking hug my kids.

CARLA. I...

You can't...

LETTIE. I can't what?

CARLA. Do that.

(*Quiet.*)

LETTIE. I can't see them?

CARLA. No, you can't...

LETTIE. What?

LETTIE.	**CARLA.**
I can't what?	They call Frank "Dad."

(*Beat.*)

CARLA. And they call me "Mom."

(*Quiet.*)

LETTIE. When, um...

When did they start...

CARLA. I don't know. We told them, a couple of years ago, we just offered and said, "If that's something you want to do, if you would like to do that then you can do that."

LETTIE. So it was something they wanted to do?

CARLA. Yes. It was. It is.

LETTIE. ...

CARLA. So, I want to make sure you know that.

(*Quiet.*)

LETTIE. I just…

    I just want to see them.

CARLA. We are trying to do…what's best for them.

LETTIE. You only let me see them twice in seven years.

CARLA. We've been over this.

    River had a very hard time with those visits, you know that. And getting out there –

LETTIE. Right.

CARLA. And you told me that was fine. That you didn't want to upset them –

CARLA.	**LETTIE.**
You didn't want them to have to go through that –	I know. I know what I said.

CARLA. So don't say that I haven't…

    You know I've done my best, keeping you posted and sending pictures. I know that Layla has –

LETTIE. Her name is Luisa.

CARLA. She likes to go by Layla, I've told you that – and she's done her best, sending you cards for holidays and all. You too, writing to them like you do. We've all done – really – we've all done the best that we –

LETTIE. Jesusfuckingchrist, just let me see them.

CARLA. Don't talk like that. Don't talk like that in front of me. I hate that, you know I hate that.

LETTIE. I'm sorry. I just want to see them. I know you know that's right. For me to see them after this long. I know you know that's right.

    …

    I'm gonna keep on believing that you're a person who does what's right. If I need to stop believing that, you go on and let me know. If I need to stop –

LETTIE.	**CARLA.**
I'm just saying you should go on and let me know.	Lettie.

CARLA. I'll talk to Frank tonight.

And I'll talk to the kids.

...

When you come to the house, when you are with them,
you can't talk like that. We are a Christian household.
You cannot talk the way you do.

LETTIE. Okay.

> *(Quiet.)*

CARLA. You have jeans? You're good?

LETTIE. Yeah.

> *(Quiet.)*

CARLA. This is hard for them.

LETTIE. I know.

CARLA. This is hard for us.

You were supposed to...

We weren't expecting this to happen right now. Not for
the next couple of years.

LETTIE. Me getting out early is not a bad thing, Carla.

CARLA. No, I'm not –

LETTIE. It's actually a good thing.

CARLA. I know, we're just trying to adjust.

LETTIE. It's a good thing for all of us. We can...

Start to heal, you know?

> *(**CARLA** looks at **LETTIE** for a while.)*

CARLA. I'll talk to everyone.

We'll figure something out.

A time for us all to see each other.

Have dinner.

LETTIE. Okay. Let's go ahead and do that. Let's figure
something out.

> *(**CARLA** slowly nods her head, gathers her
> things, and heads for the door.)*

CARLA. Okay. Yeah.

Okay.

LETTIE. Thanks.

    (**CARLA** *leaves.*)

Scene Four

(**LETTIE** *walks into the lunchroom. She has on
an old t-shirt, jeans, slip-on shoes. She takes
a workbook and a pack of Nabs out of her
locker. She sits, eats, looks over her workbook.*)

(**MINNY** *enters, wearing sturdy coveralls. She
walks to her locker and takes her lunch out.*)

MINNY. You're gonna need better clothes.

LETTIE. ...

MINNY. You gotta cover your feet and your arms.
   You got boots?

LETTIE. I'm fine.

MINNY. Now that you're in there, starting to work with all
   that shit, you can't wear stuff like that.

MINNY.	LETTIE.
You're gonna hurt yourself.	I'm fine.

MINNY. Also, you're no good at it so you gotta be / extra
   careful –

LETTIE. What? What makes you –

MINNY. The guy training you on the floor been talking shit,
   saying how you're all sloppy.
   Saying you're gonna burn the place down.

LETTIE. I'll get it, all right?
   Jesus. It's just fucking new and then I'll get it.

      (*Beat.*)

MINNY. You getting used to it?

LETTIE. I thought so, but I guess everybody thinks I suck at
   it –

MINNY. Nah not welding.
   The world.

LETTIE. Oh.
   Yeah. I guess.
   I mean, it's the world.
   Not like I'm from outer space or some shit.

MINNY. Well, you're in the real world after being locked up for ten years.

LETTIE. Seven.

MINNY. You're like E.T. or some shit.

You don't know this place.

LETTIE. It's not like –

MINNY. Naw, not E.T. because people loved him, right?

Like, "Oh shit, that alien is weird cute! I can get behind that little thing."

You ain't even like a cool scary alien, like, "Damn I can't stop looking because that alien is mad terrifying."

No, you're the alien that – you're like the alien that's like a brown mold plant thing.

It's like a living, breathing thing on another planet so it sort of counts as an alien, but ain't nobody care about it.

LETTIE. Thanks?

MINNY. Yo, I'm sorry.

LETTIE. No, it's cool. I'm mold. That's cool.

MINNY. No, I'm mold too! I'm saying it like – I didn't mean it like...

...

Toilets that flush by themselves?

Without you having to do nothing?

That freaked me out.

I was like, "Shit, are there machines somewhere out there that wipe your ass, too?" And phones. Getting used to all this phone shit. You got one?

LETTIE. No. Not yet.

MINNY. I got a shit one. But. Yeah.

I was tripping when I first got out. Still am.

But those first few weeks...

LETTIE. Well, Spring House is sort of...

It's not like the real world, you know?

That place is busted, but they're all up on me with rules, curfews, chores and shit.

Ain't like I got, like, actual freedom.

MINNY. Oh, yeah. Well, people are always gonna be on you.

LETTIE. I'm gonna get my own spot. Then, you know.

MINNY. You don't have family you can stay with?

LETTIE. Nah.

MINNY. Two?

LETTIE. What?

MINNY. That's how many kids you got?

LETTIE. Yeah. Boy and a girl.

> *(Quiet.)*

MINNY. I had one.

LETTIE. Oh yeah? Where –

MINNY. You get to see 'em yet?

LETTIE. No.

MINNY. They stay with your sister, yeah?

LETTIE. Yeah.

MINNY. They know you, right?

LETTIE. Yeah. It's been a minute.
    But they know me.

MINNY. They know you're their mom?

LETTIE. Yeah. They know that.

MINNY. You're gonna get them back? You wanna do that,
    yeah?

LETTIE. Yeah. I told you that.

MINNY. When?

LETTIE. When what?

MINNY. When you gonna get 'em back?

LETTIE. Soon.
    I'm figuring some stuff out and then –

MINNY. You keep saying that: "Soon."
    When is soon?

LETTIE. What?

MINNY. When? When is soon?

LETTIE. What the fuck do you mean "When is soon?"

MINNY. Yo, I'm just trying to talk –

LETTIE. Yeah, trying to talk –

Telling me that everyone here thinks I'm a fucking idiot?

MINNY. I didn't say that –

LETTIE. Telling me that I'm fucking mold that nobody wants to fucking look at?

Telling me how to act, how to dress –

MINNY. I don't want you walking out of here looking like a fucking melted candle.

I'm trying to be your friend here, to help you out.

LETTIE. I don't need your help.

Telling me what to do like you're my mom or some shit.

I don't need you telling me nothing.

MINNY. All I'm trying to do is act like a normal person.

I'm trying to be a real fucking person.

All I got time for is good things.

I was trying to have a nice talk with you.

I was trying to be fucking friendly.

Well fuck that.

(She leaves.)

Scene Five

(**CARLA** *leads* **LETTIE** *through her front door
into her house, car keys in hand. She has on
an IHOP uniform.*)

CARLA. Frank!

(**LETTIE** *looks around Carla's house. There's a
lot of Jesus stuff. She picks up a cutesy glass
angel from a shelf.*)

NO!

Sorry, no.

It's Layla's –

That's the first thing she bought me with her own
money. She used her allowance and her dad took her to
a dollar store, some store like that and she picked that
out. Frank!

(**LETTIE** *stops at a double frame displaying
school pictures of River and Layla.*)

LETTIE. I'm not gonna pick it up.

Just looking.

CARLA. Oh. No. You can –

Of course.

LETTIE. These are from this year?

CARLA. Yes. I was just about to send them to you. But then…
You know, here you are! So. No sense in mailing them
to…

Layla was so mad that school pictures happened two
weeks before she got her braces removed. Look, she's
not even smiling.

LETTIE. So, Layla. That's like officially her name now?

CARLA. That's what she goes by, you knew that.

LETTIE. I thought it was just…

I didn't know it / was like –

CARLA. No. Yeah. That's what everybody calls her. I like it.

LETTIE. What about River?

You let him keep his name?

CARLA. I, um...

I didn't make...

LETTIE. I'm joking.

CARLA. FRANK!

He should be here. With them.

He knew I had to go get you right after work and that I wouldn't have time to –

I just moved from part-time to full-time at IHOP and we're still –

Frank was gonna get them and dinner and –

> (**RIVER** *enters from the front door.*)

Hey! Where are you coming from?

RIVER. Jason's.

CARLA. You decided not to go with them? To the Jewel?

> (**RIVER** *shrugs, "No."*)

Um, so. I told you that we're gonna have dinner tonight. With Lettie.

> (*Beat.*)

LETTIE. Hey.

RIVER. Hey.

LETTIE. Long time no see.

You look great. I like your hair.

RIVER. Okay. It's just hair.

LETTIE. You got a style going on. I like it.

CARLA. I'm gonna go and call Frank. See where they are.

> (*She goes to the kitchen.* **RIVER** *begins walking to his room.*)

LETTIE. Hey, I uh –

Carlz said you were real into records. Collecting them.

RIVER. Yeah.

LETTIE. So, I just got this.

(Pulling an old funk record out of her bag.)

LETTIE. For you. It's old school, but I thought it'd be fun.
Just to have. Just to listen to.

(She holds the record out for **RIVER**. *It takes him a minute to take it from her.)*

RIVER. Um, yeah. I don't...
I mean I've never even heard of this group. Or band or whatever.

LETTIE. Yeah, no, it just looked cool. Like a funky old cover, so I thought...
I just got that one, but maybe we can go to the store sometime.
You can pick some out and...
I'll get 'em for ya.

RIVER. Where do you live?

LETTIE. Near West Side.

RIVER. Carlz said it was like a shelter or something.

LETTIE. It's not like...you know it's a spot for people, women, just getting out.
You call her Carlz?

RIVER. Huh?

LETTIE. That's what you call...
Carlz?

RIVER. Yeah. That's always been like...

(Shrugs, "Who cares?")

Do you have a job?

LETTIE. Yeah. Yeah.
Well, I'm in a training program. For a job.
But the program pays you to train and then the job is real good.
Everything is going really well, you know me being back, it's been going –

RIVER. What is it?

LETTIE. What?

RIVER. The job?

LETTIE. Welding.

RIVER. What?

LETTIE. Welding.

RIVER. Like, metal?

LETTIE. Yeah, like metal.

RIVER. In a factory or something?

LETTIE. Yeah. Maybe.

Start with that, you know.

Then something else.

RIVER. Like what?

LETTIE. Huh?

RIVER. Like, what's the something else?

LETTIE. All kinds of...

You know, start there and then see.

But hey. Hey man.

> *(She tries to hug* **RIVER.** *He lets her but it's not great.)*

> *(From the kitchen, we hear* **CARLA.***)*

CARLA. *(To* **FRANK.***)* There you are!

I was trying to call you.

You got it all?

FRANK. Where is she?

CARLA. In the front with River.

LAYLA. She's here?

CARLA. I told you, I told you both that she would be so put that down and go say –

I'll get it, just go say "hello" please.

> *(***FRANK** *marches to the front door/hallway.)*

FRANK. Lettie. Hey there.

LETTIE. Hey Frank.

FRANK. How's the job?

LETTIE. It's a training program.

But. It's good.

> (**LAYLA** *enters from the kitchen.* **LETTIE** *takes a long look at her.*)

LAYLA. Hey.

LETTIE. Hey. Luisa. Look at you.

LAYLA. Oh you can just call me Layla.

It's like, what I go by.

LETTIE. Okay. Layla.

> (**LAYLA** *shrugs, walks to* **LETTIE**, *and very easily gives her a quick hug.* **LETTIE** *pulls a little stuffed turtle out of her bag and hands it to* **LAYLA**.)

I know you're too old for stuffed animals, but it was the only thing I could find that was like…"turtle."

You used to be obsessed with turtles, so I just…thought you'd like that.

LAYLA. Thanks. It's cute.

CARLA. *(From the kitchen.)* Okay! Who's hungry?

> *(She peaks her head into the front room.)*

Frank, River, Layla, table now please!

Lettie, come on. This'll be nice, it'll be really nice.

Scene Six

> *(LETTIE, CARLA, FRANK, RIVER, and LAYLA all sit around the table, passing around food from a grocery store deli. The food still stays in styrofoam containers, but they eat off real plates.)*

FRANK. River, you wanna bless the food?

LAYLA. I will.

FRANK. You always do it. Wanted to give your brother a chance –

RIVER. She can do it.

CARLA. River. I'd love it if you –

RIVER. I don't want to. Layla. Go.

> *(LAYLA clasps her hands in prayer and closes her eyes. She speaks with passion...the blessing is a dramatic monologue.)*

LAYLA. Lord God and Giver of All Good Gifts,
We are grateful as we pause before this meal
For all the blessings of life that You give to us.
Daily, we are fed with good things,
Nourished by friendship and care,
Feasted with forgiveness and understanding.
And so, mindful of Your continuous care,
We pause to be grateful for the blessings of this table.

> *(She pauses and closes her eyes extra tight. LETTIE opens her eyes and looks around the table, "Is it over?")*

May your presence be the "extra" taste to this meal which we eat in the name of Your Son,
Jesus. Amen.

ALL. Amen.

CARLA. This looks good.

FRANK. It does.

CARLA. I thought this would be nice.

    To get all this, all kinds of stuff, as a special – you know to make it a more special dinner.

    To say, "Welcome back." Just more fun like this, I think.

LETTIE. That's nice. Thanks Carla.

LAYLA. Lettie, I am obsessed with mac and cheese.

LETTIE. Oh yeah?

FRANK. Well, we got plenty of it.

LAYLA. Did they only feed you bologna sandwiches in jail?

CARLA. Layla.

LETTIE. Nah. We had a master chef up in there.

    Making us whatever we wanted.

    Sushi and shit.

CARLA. Lettie.

LETTIE. What?

LAYLA. You said "shit."

CARLA. Layla.

LAYLA. What? I'm just telling her why you're freaking out.

LETTIE. Nah. My bad.

    That's on me. My bad.

        (She wants to try and talk, to ask questions, but has a hard time knowing how to start.)

LAYLA. Lettie, I'm playing Pepper in *Annie*.

LETTIE. Oh, shit!

CARLA. Lettie!

LETTIE. Sorry.

    (To **LAYLA.***)* That's like a big part, right? Pepper?

    She's the one who's sort of an asshole, yeah?

LAYLA. *(Giggling.)* Yeah.

FRANK. Lettie, I need to ask you to watch your language here in our house.

    Cool?

LETTIE. What?

FRANK. Are we cool with the language?

LETTIE. Yeah. Yeah Frank.

We're cool.

So, like the school play?

CARLA. Yes. Layla worked very hard on her audition.

She beat out, what? How many other girls auditioned for that part?

LAYLA. I don't remember.

CARLA. It was competitive. She's good.

LAYLA. I wanna be an actress.

LETTIE. Yeah, in your last letter you said that. I think you were trying to decide between actress and like governor or something?

LAYLA. Yeah! Politician. But it's officially actress now. For sure.

CARLA. She's very talented but grades first, because even if she wants to be an actress, she wants to be smart. She doesn't want to be a dumb actress.

FRANK. Layla is smart.

LETTIE. She's always been smart.

LAYLA. Do you have a tattoo?

LETTIE. Uh. Yeah.

Yeah, I got a tattoo.

LAYLA. Did you get it in prison?

LETTIE. Nah. I already had it from before.

LAYLA. Oooh, can I see?

CARLA. We're at the table, Layla.

LAYLA. I'm dying to get one.

RIVER. So dumb.

LAYLA. As soon as I'm eighteen I'm getting one.

FRANK. Just don't ever let me see it.

LAYLA. On my ankle.

LETTIE. What are you gonna get? Do you know?

LAYLA. Yes! It's gonna –

CARLA. I'd rather not hear about it.

LETTIE. Oh.

LAYLA. I'll tell you later.

FRANK. So. Lettie. Your new job. Is it full / time –

LETTIE. It's a training program.

FRANK. Right. It's every day?

LETTIE. Not weekends.

But, yeah.

FRANK. Nine to five? Like a job?

LETTIE. Yeah. Got a timecard and everything.

FRANK. They pay you?

LETTIE. A little. Yeah.

FRANK. But it's a training program?

LETTIE. Yeah.

FRANK. So, you get paid to train with them?

LETTIE. It's part of the re-entry / program.

FRANK. They pay you?

LETTIE. *(Beat.)* Yeah.

FRANK. Shoot. I had to pay for my training.

Had to take out a loan for it, actually.

I should've looked into finding a way to be a part of this re-entry stuff.

LETTIE. You should definitely look into it.

I can't recommend prison and then re-entry highly enough.

FRANK. I was…

My training cost me a lot of money.

Could've used that money for River's college fund.

LETTIE. Oh, wow.

College.

FRANK. Yep.

LETTIE. You're already talking about that stuff?

FRANK. He's seventeen. So yes.

We are.

We're gonna figure out something.

CARLA. We will.

LETTIE. *(To* **RIVER**.*)* Uh, where do you –
Do you know where you wanna go? What kind of job you want?

FRANK. Anything other than what I do.
Isn't that right, River?

RIVER. I just –
Don't wanna be in a factory.

FRANK. I don't blame you.

LETTIE. Oh. Frank, Carla was always saying that you liked your job.
You're a manager?

CARLA. Operations Supervisor.

LETTIE. That it's a good job. Right? That you felt lucky you got to do –

FRANK. Lucky?
No. I'm not feeling particularly lucky at the moment.

> *(A laugh from him.)*

LETTIE. *(Looking down at her plate.)* So, school is going good?

> *(A look around the table, "Who is she talking to?"* **LETTIE** *keeps her head down, eating.)*

CARLA. Who are you talking to?
About school going well?

LETTIE. Uh...whoever wants to answer, I guess.

LAYLA. School's great except for the classes.

LETTIE. Ha!

CARLA. She made straight A's – well, one B – but straight A's pretty much.

LETTIE. Oh yeah?

FRANK. Yep. She's doing real good.

LAYLA. I love after-school stuff.
I do drama, cheerleading, student council, soccer, speech and debate.
I just literally like to do everything.

LETTIE. Makes sense. I did too.

CARLA. But she makes good grades.

LETTIE. Oh, yeah. Nah.

I didn't do that.

CARLA. I told her as long as her grades are good she can do whatever she wants.

LAYLA. *(Re:* **CARLA**.*)* Yeah, she like has to drive me everywhere because I always have to be at something.

It's like she has work and then drive Layla everywhere work.

CARLA. I don't mind. Gives her a chance to keep me up to speed on what's cool.

(**LAYLA** *starts laughing.*)

What?

LAYLA. River, yesterday she tried to sing that new Rihanna song.

CARLA. I like that song!

RIVER. That's like, a pretty dirty song.

CARLA. They don't play the dirty version on the radio!

It's all bleeped out!

LAYLA. I was dying laughing.

CARLA. You were impressed I knew the lyrics. I could tell you were.

LAYLA. No, I totally was.

(*Beat.*)

LETTIE. You guys gotta get me into all the stuff. You know, music, all the stuff that's in.

(*Beat.*)

That's awesome. That you make good grades.

And all your stuff. All the stuff that you do.

LAYLA. You dropped out, right?

LETTIE.	**CARLA**.
Yeah. Stupid.	Layla.

LAYLA. Why?

LETTIE. *(Shrugs.)* Just. Wasn't for me.

It's a long story, but –

FRANK. And now you're getting paid to go to school. Right? Worked out.

CARLA. No one should drop out of / high school –

LETTIE. *(With a laugh.)* I wouldn't say it "worked out."

FRANK. You wouldn't?

> *(Beat.)*

LETTIE. River, you got a subject that –

RIVER. No.

CARLA. Computers. You're good with that.

LETTIE. But you make music?

That's, like, what you're passionate about, right?

That's what you really want to do?

FRANK. I don't know how collecting a bunch of records adds up to being someone who makes music.

Feels like you gotta actually make music to be someone who makes music.

RIVER. I wanna be a producer. So it actually does add up –

LETTIE. Oh, cool.

FRANK. Sitting in your room with the door shut listening to records? That's producing? That's a job?

Shoot, sign me up.

RIVER. I told you, there's a lot that goes into it –

FRANK. And I've told you to show me the scholarship for that and I'll get behind it 100 percent.

CARLA. *(To* **LETTIE**.*)* River can get on a computer and just know exactly what to do. He's so good with them.

LETTIE. Right.

So, like being a producer, like you try to find –

RIVER. Can we talk about something else?

LETTIE. Oh. I think it's cool. I'm just trying to figure out what it –

FRANK. He collects records and it's a hobby.
I'm all for it, I think it's a fun thing.

RIVER. I'm done.

CARLA. River. Sit down.

RIVER. I'm done. I'm good.

(He leaves the room.)

FRANK. I just want to talk about jobs like they're jobs and hobbies like they're hobbies.

LETTIE. He's seventeen.

FRANK. So?

LETTIE. So. I guess...like, just let him...
I don't know.

FRANK. Just let him what?

LETTIE. I guess, just...

FRANK. Not care? Just let him do whatever he wants?

CARLA. Frank.

FRANK. Sorry. I'm just trying to clarify.

LETTIE. What's wrong with you, man?

FRANK. Excuse me?

LETTIE. It's like... I don't know. Like, you're making everybody uncomfortable.

FRANK. I'm making everybody uncomfortable?

LETTIE. Yeah. Just like... I don't know. Relax.

FRANK. Oh. Relax. Okay. Great idea. Thanks. Thank you, Lettie.

LETTIE. Okay. I'm gonna go ahead and go.

LAYLA. No!

LETTIE. Yeah, I gotta get back.

CARLA. Lettie.

LETTIE. I'm gonna grab the bus. But thanks for dinner, Carla.
(Hugging **LAYLA.***)* I'll see you soon, okay?

(She heads for the door.)

CARLA. Wait.

LETTIE. Nah. It's all good. I just... I'm gonna just get back.

> *(She leaves.)*

FRANK. That temper of hers seems to be alive and well, huh?

LAYLA. You were rude.

FRANK. Excuse me?

LAYLA.	**CARLA.**
You weren't very nice to her.	Please. Can we just –

FRANK. I wasn't nice to her?

CARLA. Frank.

FRANK. You wanna talk about how I haven't been "nice" to her?

> (**LAYLA** *stands up.*)

LAYLA. I'm done.

FRANK. Sit down.

LAYLA. I'm. Done.

> *(She storms out.)*
>
> *(Quiet.)*

FRANK. I'm sorry.

CARLA. It's okay.

FRANK. I'm...

I just don't know what...

CARLA. I know.

FRANK. I don't know how to be around her.

CARLA. I know.

FRANK. I'm sorry.

I can't even look her in the eye.

I can't.

CARLA. It's okay. We just got a lot thrown at us and it's...

Well, it's just a hard time.

FRANK. Yeah.

CARLA. We'll get through it.

FRANK. I heard from Termaxx today. The job's not going my way. But, the supervisor was nice enough to call me himself and let me know.

CARLA. Oh, I'm sorry, honey.

FRANK. The title was the same one I've had for the past twenty years, but now the job is totally different.

There's a lot more to it with new technology and all that.

A whole other thing than when I first started.

CARLA. But you can learn. You can learn all the new stuff.

FRANK. Well, no one wants to hire a guy so that he can learn.

CARLA. It's gonna work out.

FRANK. I have an interview with Uline tomorrow, one with Orbis on Thursday.

CARLA. Something will come through.

FRANK. I hope so. But...

It's not looking so good.

It's just not looking so good.

CARLA. We're gonna be okay. With the job, with the kids.

We're gonna keep praying and trying and hoping and that's it.

That's all we can do.

FRANK. I'm sorry...

If I was rude to Lettie.

CARLA. It's okay.

FRANK. I'm sorry.

CARLA. I know, honey.

FRANK. Oh boy. I don't know what to do.

> (**CARLA** *reaches across the table and pats* **FRANK**'s *hand.*)

I really just don't know what to do.

Scene Seven

(**LETTIE** *runs into the lunchroom, holding her arm, wincing in pain.*)

LETTIE. Fuck.

(**MINNY** *enters with her welding mask on. She takes it off and heads to a cabinet. She gets out a first-aid kit, opens it, pulls out a tube of burn cream, and goes to* **LETTIE** *at the sink.*)

MINNY. Let me see it.

LETTIE. It's cool.

(**MINNY** *grabs her arm and examines it.*)

MINNY. Got you good.

LETTIE. Yeah.

MINNY. You wanna go to the hospital?

LETTIE. Nah. I don't know.

MINNY. Aight.

Just gonna put this on your burn.

LETTIE. Thanks.

(**MINNY** *gently spreads the cream on* **LETTIE**'s *burn.*)

Sorry about the other day.

(*Nodding to* **MINNY**'s *coveralls.*) Looks like I gotta get me one of those suits.

MINNY. They have used ones here.

You can borrow them.

(*She begins wrapping* **LETTIE**'s *burn with gauze.*)

LETTIE. I can see why that old lady liked you.

You know the one you took care of?

You're good at...

Like a nurse or some shit.

MINNY. My ex-husband held my baby's feet down on the radiator.

Third-degree burn.

Had to take her to the emergency room.

Wrapped those little feet for weeks.

> *(Beat.)*

LETTIE. You had a daughter?

MINNY. Second time he did that they took her away from
me.

> *(Quiet.)*

LETTIE. You kill him?

MINNY. Yeah.

Wish I could've done it more than once.

> *(Beat.)*

LETTIE. I was in for drugs, trafficking and shit.

I was all fucked up. For a long time, I was just...

But.

MINNY. ...

LETTIE. I'm sorry.

About what I said –

MINNY. You already told me "sorry."

LETTIE. Yeah, but I'm telling you / again –

MINNY. I'm not trying to be your friend.

You burned your arm.

I know how to treat a burn.

That's it.

> *(She grabs her mask and leaves.)*

Scene Eight

> (**LETTIE** *rushes into the common room at Spring House.* **LAYLA** *is there.*)

LETTIE. Whoa!

LAYLA. Hey.

LETTIE. I wasn't expecting you –
   Otherwise, I would've...

> (*She hugs* **LAYLA**.)

   But I'm so glad!
   Hey!

LAYLA. Hey.

LETTIE. Did Carla bring you, or –

LAYLA. I took the bus. A couple of buses.

LETTIE. They know you're here?

LAYLA. It's fine. It's cool.

LETTIE. Okay. Um –

LAYLA. What happened to your arm?

LETTIE. Oh, I burned it, it's fine.
   You want like a snack or something?
   I can go to the vending machine. They got Ruffles, Oreos –

LAYLA. I can't eat Oreos.

LETTIE. You can't eat Oreos?
   What the hell is wrong with you?

LAYLA. My dad. Frank, that's the company he works for –

LETTIE. Oh, yeah.
   Right.

LAYLA. When he first started there, we ate them all the time. Like, birthday cake and stuff? We ate Oreos. It was dessert, snack, everything. One time I ate so many that I barfed everywhere and now I literally can't even look at them.

LETTIE. Okay. So.

No Oreos.

LAYLA. Can I see your room?

LETTIE. We can't have guests in the rooms. Just out here.

Man, I wish you could see it because you know what I got covering the wall next to my bed?

LAYLA. What?

LETTIE. The cards you sent me. For holidays and stuff. And pictures of you and River, but your cards take up the most room.

LAYLA. You kept those?

LETTIE. Of course I did.

LAYLA. They were just like, I don't know...

Stupid cards.

LETTIE. I love them.

LAYLA. Does your arm hurt?

LETTIE. Nah.

LAYLA. It happened at your training thing?

LETTIE. Yeah.

LAYLA. Are you gonna make jewelry?

LETTIE. What?

LAYLA. Welding. I looked it up and you can make jewelry.

LETTIE. Nah. I'm probably just gonna make a part for some machine in some factory.

LAYLA. Do you like it? Welding?

LETTIE. Nah, not really.

LAYLA. Then, why are you doing it?

LETTIE. For a job.

LAYLA. Right. But, why not do something else?

LETTIE. Yeah, no, this is just for now but then something else, for sure.

At least I don't have to wear a skirt and heels to work.

LAYLA. Oh my god, I love heels.

LETTIE. Yeah. Not me.

LAYLA. But I remember... I remember you used to wear heels. Like, all the time.

LETTIE. Yeah?

LAYLA. Yeah, I would get so excited when I heard clomp-clomp-clomp, like, "Here she comes!"

And makeup. You always had it on. Even to go to bed.

LETTIE. Yeah. I was into that for a while.

LAYLA. I love all that.

LETTIE. Yeah, I mean if you're gonna be an actress, I guess you better.

LAYLA. Do you think we look alike?

You and River look alike.

Do I look more like my dad?

Like, my dad dad?

LETTIE. Yeah. You do.

LAYLA. He's in Texas?

LETTIE. Last I heard.

LAYLA. He's in jail?

LETTIE. Last I heard.

LAYLA. I have like, so many questions. And now that you're... Well, I didn't want to ask you all this stuff on like a Christmas card –

LETTIE. Yeah. Yeah. We can talk about...

But I'm sure you know most of it. Carla and Frank have probably told you –

LAYLA. They don't tell me anything.

Just that me and River have two different dads. But, duh. And that you and my mom have two different dads. And that you guys's mom left her and her dad to be with your dad and then she had you and was never around and even though my mom got the shit end of the deal, she still managed to stay out of trouble.

LETTIE. Well. You know. That's one version. I guess.

Thought you weren't allowed to say "shit."

LAYLA. I'm not.

But I'm with you.

LETTIE. You think that I don't care about you cursing?

LAYLA. I didn't...

LETTIE. Well. You should know...

That I really don't give a shit.

LAYLA. You're a jerk!

LETTIE. I don't give a fuck!

LAYLA. Oh my god!

> *(Beat.)*

It was drugs, right?

LETTIE. Um, what?

LAYLA. You bought them and you sold them?

> **(LETTIE** *stays looking down and gives a small nod, "Yes.")*

And you did them, right? You were...addicted to them?

LETTIE. Yeah. It was all pretty complicated / you know?

LAYLA. That's why you kept messing / up.

LETTIE. You know, it was a long time ago.

I had a problem.

But it's all good now.

LAYLA. Why wasn't it then?

LETTIE. Um. I tried real hard. Then something would happen and I would be right back at the beginning. And then everything all over again. It was like...

I couldn't escape.

LAYLA. Couldn't escape what?

LETTIE. Me. I guess.

> *(Beat.)*

LAYLA. I remember you used to let me eat hot dogs for breakfast.

I remember some mornings I would come in the kitchen and you would say, "Let's have a cookout!" and it would be like, seven in the morning.

LETTIE. Yeah?

LAYLA. And I remember you let me get all those hermit crabs when I was like, six.

Remember? At the pet store?

I wanted a little turtle but all they had were hermit crabs and I was like, "I want one."

And you were like, "Well, then let's get ten."

Mom and Dad were pissed.

LETTIE. We were living with Carla and Frank, then? When you were six?

LAYLA. I mean, you were in and out.

Can I see your tattoo?

LETTIE. You never seen it?

LAYLA. No.

LETTIE. I've had it for a while. You definitely saw it when you were little.

LAYLA. I don't remember. Please?

> (**LETTIE** *lowers her shirt and above her heart is a tattoo that reads: "Luisa and River.")*

No way! "Luisa and River."

LETTIE. Yup.

LAYLA. Awesome.

LETTIE. So, no one calls you Luisa anymore?

LAYLA. It's, like, old lady.

LETTIE. What?

LAYLA. Luisa is. It's an old lady name.

Layla is good, just like a nickname.

LETTIE. Okay.

So, how's the play going? *Annie*? You know all your lines?

LAYLA. My biological dad, he's 100 percent Mexican right?

LETTIE. He's 100 percent motherfucker, I can fucking tell you that.

…

Shit, I'm sorry.

LAYLA. I don't care. It's not like I know him or anything.

LETTIE. Right, just. I shouldn't –

LAYLA. He's Mexican, though?

LETTIE. Yeah, uh...he was from Mexico, but he moved to Texas when he was a little kid.

LAYLA. So, I can date a Puerto Rican guy? Right?

LETTIE. Uh...

You can date whoever you want.

But you know, you're fourteen.

LAYLA. I have a boyfriend.

LETTIE. Oh. Cool. Okay.

LAYLA. And my dad hates it.

LETTIE. Well, you know. Frank's probably just looking out for you.

Worried, you know?

LAYLA. He says, "He doesn't like Ian's kind."

LETTIE. Oh. He, like, a thug or something?

LAYLA. No. Dad won't say he doesn't like him because he's Puerto Rican, but I know that's what he means when he says "Ian's kind." He hates Mexicans, Puerto Ricans –

LETTIE. What? What do you mean?

LAYLA. Whenever we have to fill out forms, like for the doctor or school, I check "Other."

I was applying to go to this drama festival and he saw my application on the kitchen table and made me change it from "Other" to "White." I like that I'm "Other."

Don't you? Like that I'm "Other"?

LETTIE. Yeah. Yes.

LAYLA. I joke with him, like, "Don't you know I'll get more opportunities, like scholarships and stuff, if I check 'Other'?!" And he gets so pissed.

Do you want to see his picture?

LETTIE. Huh?

LAYLA. Ian's?

LETTIE. Um, yeah. Sure.

(**LAYLA** *gets out her phone and shows* **LETTIE** *a picture.*)

LAYLA. That's him. Isn't he cute?

He's so cute.

LETTIE. Yeah.

I know it's not –

I'm not trying to get in your business but –

You're being careful?

LAYLA. I'm a virgin.

I'm gonna stay a virgin until I'm sixteen.

LETTIE. Oh.

LAYLA. I know you didn't.

LETTIE. What?

LAYLA. Like, wait. The math, like...is sort of clear.

River, you, / the math –

LETTIE. Yeah. No. It's...

Just. Like I said. Be careful.

LAYLA. I know! I'm not an idiot.

Oh my god, let's take a picture! Okay, we're totally taking a picture.

(She holds her phone for a picture. She is great with selfies, **LETTIE** *is not.)*

That's so cute! Look!

LETTIE. Wow. Yeah.

Can I get a copy of that?

LAYLA. Yeah. I'll text you. Oh my god, I don't even have your phone number.

LETTIE. Yeah, I don't have a phone just yet.

LAYLA. What?

LETTIE. I'm getting one soon, and then, yeah.

You can just text it to me.

...

Hey. I have an idea.

LAYLA. What?

LETTIE. Let's go get hot dogs.

Scene Nine

(LETTIE and LAYLA walk up to the house, CARLA runs out to meet them.)

CARLA. *(To LAYLA.)* Where have you been? Why haven't you been answering your phone?

(To LETTIE.) Why didn't you make her answer her phone?

LAYLA. I had it on "Do Not Disturb."

CARLA. You knew we –

Why didn't you tell us where you were?

LAYLA. Because.

We were just hanging out.

LETTIE. Sorry, Carlz. I didn't know you were trying –

CARLA. No? You didn't ask if her parents knew where she was?

If we might be worried about her?

It seems like a thing you would just – I don't know – think to ask a fourteen-year-old girl.

LAYLA. Mom, chill. It's not even ten o'clock.

CARLA. Inside. Now.

First thing you do is apologize to your father. He's been worried sick.

LETTIE. Sorry. I didn't know she had it on whatever – with her phone –

CARLA. You can't pull this crap, Lettie.

LETTIE. What?

CARLA. It is almost ten o'clock on a school night.

You kept her out with God knows who / doing God knows what –

LETTIE. We got hot dogs.

That's it.

Don't worry, we didn't fuck any 'spies while we were out.

(Beat.)

CARLA. Excuse me?

LETTIE. Yeah, she told me how you and Frank feel about all that.

That's great, Carla.

Pull that racist bullshit with a kid who's Mexican.

CARLA. She's not / Mexican.

LETTIE. Half-Mexican, whatever the fuck.

CARLA. What are you even talking about?

LETTIE. She said that you guys make her check "White" in the fucking boxes, that Frank makes her check "White." That you guys are fucking racist.

What is that?

CARLA. First of all, I'm not racist, Frank's not racist, this is a Christian household –

LETTIE. Making her check those boxes "White." Do you know how messed up that is?

CARLA. Did it ever occur to you that he's trying to be close to her when he does that?

That he's saying, "No. No. DNA doesn't matter. I'm your father and you are a part of this family."

LETTIE. No. That never occurred to me.

(**FRANK** *comes to the door, puts his arm around* **CARLA.**)

FRANK. Okay. Lettie. That's enough.

LETTIE. Oh, I got a bone to pick with you, man –

FRANK. It's ten o'clock –

FRANK.	**LETTIE.**
– On a school night and you're screaming at my wife at the front door of my house.	It's not even ten yet! Jesus!
That's enough.	

LETTIE. Naw, see, you can't tell me what to do, Frank. That's not what's gonna happen here.

CARLA. Okay, both of you. Please, let's –

FRANK. You're not gonna keep my child out, then come –

LETTIE. Your child?

FRANK. – Here and scream obscenities at my wife. This is not the kind of life that we lead and we're not gonna let you –

LETTIE. You're not gonna let me do what? Huh? What exactly aren't you gonna let me do?

CARLA. Please.

LETTIE. What aren't you gonna let me do?

(She gets right up in FRANK's face. Ready.)

You tell me what you aren't gonna let me do.

FRANK. Get off my porch, Lettie.

LETTIE. Make me, you old fuck.

CARLA. That's enough. You hear me? That's enough.

LETTIE. Nah, the two of you can't tell me what I can and –

FRANK. Goodnight, Lettie.

*(He slams the front door shut. **LETTIE** runs up to the front door and kicks it. She kicks it again. She kicks it once more, even harder, and hurts her toe.)*

LETTIE. Shit.

(She grabs her foot, wincing in pain, then yells toward the house.)

Fucking suck my dick, man!

Fuck you!

Scene Ten

(The lunchroom. **LETTIE** *sits, eating Nabs. She wears coveralls folded down at the waist, with a t-shirt and a bandage on her arm.* **MINNY** *enters, takes her mask off, and goes to her locker.)*

LETTIE. Hey.

*(***MINNY*** doesn't say anything, gets her lunch out.)*

I borrowed these.

It's better.

Stupid that I hadn't done it before.

MINNY. I didn't know you were still here.

LETTIE. Yeah. I've been...

I had to go to the doctor for the burn and he told me that, you know, I had to stay away from heat for a few days.

So, I been at Spring, doing the homework, reading the books and shit.

MINNY. You been gone a week.

LETTIE. Yeah.

MINNY. They didn't kick you out?

LETTIE. No, I...

The burn.

MINNY. Huh. Must be nice to be you.

LETTIE. The doctor told me –

MINNY. You didn't go to a doctor.

LETTIE. What?

MINNY. A doctor never would've wrapped your arm like that.

Looks like a blind three-year-old did that.

Cool though, that they didn't kick you out for missing so much.

Told you: you guys get better stuff.

LETTIE. What's your problem with me?

I'm trying to be nice –

MINNY. You got a bad attitude.

I got no room for someone with a bad attitude.

LETTIE. You don't even know me.

MINNY. I see you the way you walk around, all pissed off that life did you like this.

LETTIE. I don't walk –

MINNY. Yeah. You do. Acting like you shouldn't be here.

Thinking you don't have to do what the rest of us have to do.

Titty-Baby shit.

Fuckin' bad attitude.

...

Can I give you a piece of advice? Without you screaming at me that I'm trying to be your mom?

LETTIE. Okay.

MINNY. Stop pretending you got some other life waiting for you and be realistic: "This is how shit turned out. I can either get pissed every day and tear shit apart or I can just know that this is how shit is. This is my life."

Then put your head down and fucking go to work.

LETTIE. But, like, I never...

It's never been like, my life.

I ain't ever had a say.

I never had a chance to try and get what I want.

Now that I'm clean, now that I'm out, I should, right?

I should have a say, I should have a chance to –

MINNY. You should have all kinds of shit. I should, too. But the world don't work on shoulds.

    (Beat.)

LETTIE. It means "joy."

MINNY. What?

LETTIE. My name. Lettie.

You asked me what it meant.

It means "joy."

MINNY. Shut the fuck up.

LETTIE. I'm serious.

MINNY. That's fucked up.

...

So you started using?

LETTIE. Huh?

MINNY. 'Cause you never had a say?

It was the only way I could get through it.

You gotta get through this without all that.

MINNY.	**LETTIE**.
You know that, right?	No, I'm good. I know.

MINNY. And you can't be missing days, this is for real.

LETTIE. I just needed a minute.

It's been – stuff with my kids.

I fucked up and haven't been able to see them for a while and I just needed –

MINNY. A hit?

LETTIE. I didn't. I'm good.

MINNY. All right then. Stay good.

LETTIE. I am.

MINNY. It'd be fucking nice though.

Just a little weed.

LETTIE. Right?! Just a little fucking weed every now and then.

MINNY. For real.

So, Spring House? It's shit, yeah?

LETTIE. Yeah. I gotta get out of there. Somebody pissed outside my door this morning.

I should be able to get my own spot soon, though.

MINNY. But you ain't got no money?

LETTIE. Well, after the program –

LETTIE.	**MINNY**.
Once I get a job –	You think you'll be able to finish the program?

LETTIE. Yes.

And there are places for people who don't have money.

MINNY. Be realistic.

LETTIE. I am.

There are places out there.

MINNY. Well let me know when you find one of these magical, free places.

My cousin needs me out by Friday. His son is back in town and needs the room.

LETTIE. Shit.

MINNY. All good. I know that my life is staying in some room until I get kicked out.

LETTIE. Where you gonna go?

MINNY. I'll figure it out.

LETTIE. I can see if there's any space at Spring House.

MINNY. Oh, cool, you've told me such lovely things about the place. That would be great.

LETTIE. What else you gonna do, go to a shelter or something? I'll check and see if there's a spot.

MINNY. You don't need to do nothing for me just because I helped with your –

LETTIE. I know. I'm just trying to be fucking friendly.

MINNY. Yeah. Okay.

LETTIE. It'll be so fun if you come live at Spring House.

We can do yoga together.

MINNY. Fuck you.

LETTIE. I'll ask them today.

MINNY. Thanks.

Scene Eleven

(**LETTIE** *digs through records at the record store.*
RIVER *enters, doesn't see* **LETTIE**, *and starts*
digging. **LETTIE** *looks up, spots* **RIVER**, *and goes*
to him.)

LETTIE. Hey.

RIVER. Oh. Hey.

LETTIE. What are you doing way over here? It's a trek from
your house.

RIVER. I don't know.

LETTIE. Ohhhhhhh...

You can't go nowhere close to your school. To your house.

RIVER. What?

LETTIE. You had to travel across town.

Because you're skipping.

RIVER. What?

LETTIE. You're skipping school so you had to come all the
way over to Wicker Park for your record digging. Huh?

RIVER. I don't know.

LETTIE. I do. I know all the tricks, man.

RIVER. Okay.

LETTIE. I heard this was the spot for people who were real
into records and shit.

So I thought I'd look through and try to find some stuff
for you.

Wasn't expecting to run into you. That's cool, though.

I'm glad I get to see ya.

RIVER. Why aren't you at your program or whatever?

LETTIE. I guess the apple doesn't fall too far from the tree.

RIVER. What?

LETTIE. I'm skipping too.

Don't tell.

RIVER. Won't you like...

Get in trouble?

LETTIE. Nah. I can call in sick, like one day. It's fine.

RIVER. Okay.

LETTIE. And I get to see you, so good thing I did.

RIVER. ...

LETTIE. I'm sorry I haven't been able to see you guys for a while.

Frank and Carla are making shit pretty –

RIVER. It's fine. I don't care.

LETTIE. I've been calling her, trying to –

I got a phone.

(She pulls out a flip phone.)

So, if you ever just wanna talk...

Or text. We can text whenever –

RIVER. You can text on that thing?

LETTIE. Yeah. Yeah. Takes a minute.

But yeah.

So, you can give me your number and we can...

Do that.

RIVER. ...

LETTIE. I'll be able to get an apartment soon, I think.

I've been looking and I –

RIVER. Are you high?

LETTIE. What?

RIVER. Like calling in sick to work and getting high?

LETTIE. No. No. River, I've been sober for –

RIVER. I smoke weed.

LETTIE. Okay.

RIVER. I smoked a blunt right before I walked in here.

LETTIE. You, uh, gotta be careful. Don't...

RIVER. Don't what?

LETTIE. Don't get caught.

Visine.

(**RIVER** *pulls a vial of Visine from his pocket,*
"*Duh.*")

I think it's awesome that you wanna make music.

RIVER. Okay.

LETTIE. I want you to do whatever you want. Whatever
makes you happy.

RIVER. ...

LETTIE. I used to want to be a singer. People used to say I
had a nice voice, and that I had like –
That I could do that.
So, you know, music. I'm into it and –

RIVER. It's a different thing, what I do.
It's not...yeah, it's not like "singing."
The music I wanna – yeah it's a totally different thing.

LETTIE. Oh. Well. I wanna hear about it.

RIVER. ...

LETTIE. Hey. So. I know...
Do you feel like...
Do you like living with Carla and Frank?

RIVER. What?

LETTIE. I just...
I just wanna make sure you're...
I'm just asking, you know?

RIVER. Uh. Okay.

LETTIE. Like, how ya doing?

RIVER. Oh yeah. I think that ship has sailed.

LETTIE. What?

RIVER. I think it's too late for all that, you know?

LETTIE. What do you mean?

RIVER. Like, for you to be concerned about how I'm doing.

LETTIE. I'm trying to...
Be here. Now. You know?
You okay? You happy?

RIVER. I live with people who had to take me in because my mom was a junkie.

LETTIE. I'm sorry. I –

RIVER. Who never gave a shit about me and my little sister.

LETTIE. That's not true. You gotta know that I was always trying –

RIVER. That's what trying looks like?

LETTIE. River, I'm a different person now. I know I made mistakes but I'm not...

I am not those mistakes and I...

I need you to give me a second chance, here.

RIVER. Are you kidding me right now?

LETTIE. You gotta understand that all my shit had nothing to do with how much I love you –

RIVER. What about when you caught Carla and Frank's garage on fire?

RIVER.	**LETTIE.**
The garage apartment they let you stay in?	That was an accident –

RIVER. When you had some stranger come over and get high and fucking nod off with a lit cigarette?

When your seven-year-old son was asleep on the couch –

LETTIE. It was a horrible –

RIVER. Because he wanted to have a sleepover with his mom?

(He pulls his hair back to reveal a burn scar on his neck.)

This is what love looks like?

RIVER.	**LETTIE.**
Wetting the bed and waking up in the middle of the night for the next five years screaming that we had to run because there's a fire, that's what love feels like?	Baby, I'm sorry, I was a – ... Please let me show you – Let me prove to you –

RIVER. You know why I don't call Carla "Mom"?

I know you're super interested in that, so here's why: "Mom" is the fucking nastiest word in the world to me. That word makes me want to kill myself.

LETTIE. Please. Just, let me show you –

RIVER. I'm not crazy about Carlz but she's better than the fucking trash that word means.

LETTIE. We gotta work this out.

RIVER. No. We don't.

I can't believe I'm even having this conversation right now in the middle of a record store when I'm high as fuck.

LETTIE. Please give me a chance to make this right.

RIVER. Are you gonna tell them that you saw me here? That I was skipping?

LETTIE. What?

RIVER. Carlz and Frank. Are you gonna tell –

LETTIE. No. No, of course…

(**RIVER** *begins walking out of the store.*)

Hey.

RIVER. What?

LETTIE. I love you.

I swear to God I do.

(**RIVER** *leaves.*)

Scene Twelve

> *(LETTIE waits in the common room. CARLA enters, wearing her IHOP uniform shirt.)*

CARLA. Hi.

LETTIE. Hey. Thanks, uh. It's just hard for me to get to your house.

CARLA. Right. I just need to be at work by four, so.

LETTIE. Yeah. Sure.

You want a glass of water or something?

CARLA. Okay. Thanks.

> *(LETTIE goes into the hallway, we can hear a sink. She comes back with a glass of water.)*

You're not using the Brita?

> *(Beat. LETTIE walks back into the hallway. We hear the sink running for a while. She comes back in with the water glass and Brita. The Brita filters water from the sink.)*

LETTIE. You been hard to get a hold of.

CARLA. Work. I went from part-time to full-time and it's –

| **CARLA.** | **LETTIE.** |
| A tricky time. | I've been calling you. |

CARLA. A very tricky time.

LETTIE. No shit.

CARLA. Lettie. We just needed some time. We are trying to figure out the best way...

A fourteen-year-old can't be out till ten o'clock, not answering her phone, not telling her parents where she is. Frank almost called the police he was so worried.

> *(LETTIE pours the water from the Brita into CARLA's glass. Without realizing what she's doing, CARLA wipes the rim of the glass before taking a sip. LETTIE notices.)*

LETTIE. Yeah, well. Everything was cool. She was with me. Which, obviously you guys don't like.

CARLA. You should have called.

LETTIE. I don't need to check in with you and Frank, Carla.

CARLA. You don't, but Layla does.

LETTIE. Luisa.

CARLA. What?

LETTIE. Did Frank change her name?

CARLA. Lettie.

LETTIE. I'm just asking.

CARLA. No, Layla is a nickname and –

LETTIE. But who started calling her that? Like, as a / nickname?

CARLA. Frank's a good dad to them. What you said about him – about me – wasn't fair. We love them very much. You know that.

And we've done the best that we can with all of this.

LETTIE. Yeah, yeah. I appreciate what you've done, looking after them. I do.

CARLA. We're not "looking after them" –

LETTIE. Yeah. You are. Temporary Guardianship. That's the form we filled out.

CARLA. What?

LETTIE. But I'm ready to go ahead and move forward.

CARLA. And we will all figure out how to do that, together.

LETTIE. I'm their mom.

So, *we* don't actually have to figure it out together.

CARLA. ...

LETTIE. I'm gonna get a job and an apartment and I want River and Luisa –

CARLA. Layla.

LETTIE. To live with me. It's time, you know? For us to be together, to be a family.

Like I said, I appreciate everything –

CARLA. You're serious? You're serious right now?

LETTIE. I'm their mom.

CARLA. You honestly think you can just come back, after all this time, after all your mistakes and say, "I'm ready to be a mom now" and then – boom – you're a mom? Is that what you think?

LETTIE. Yeah.

CARLA. Okay. Well, I'm here to tell you that you don't get to do that.

LETTIE. That agreement we signed tells me that I do.

CARLA. This takes time, Lettie. Have you thought about River and Layla and –

LETTIE. Don't ask me if I've thought about them –

CARLA. It's a valid question.

LETTIE. River is gonna go to college and never know that I'm his mother – that I'm his mother in a real way – and you're gonna keep Layla away from me –

CARLA. No, I won't.

LETTIE. You'll keep doing this shit, saying we'll get to it later and it takes time and it has to be gradual and then they'll keep getting farther and farther away and then they'll both be gone. I need a fucking chance to be their mom and you are gonna keep –

CARLA. I told you, we will figure it out.

LETTIE. But you're lying.

You thought I was gonna stay in and just keep fucking up and then we would never have to figure it out. They would just be your kids and I would fucking fade away, I would fucking rot. That's what you've been doing this whole –

CARLA. Are you kidding me? Are you actually –

LETTIE. But I made it. I made it and I'm here and I'm good and I want my kids back.

CARLA. No.

LETTIE. What?

CARLA. No.

LETTIE. I don't know what you...

Carla... I never gave you custody.

I mean, I appreciate you taking care of them for the last seven years –

CARLA. We have taken care of them for seventeen years, Lettie, not seven.

And we are happy to because we love them –

(**LETTIE** *scoffs.*)

Don't you dare! You have no idea how hard we have worked.

You have no idea what we have given up for them.

For you.

LETTIE. You fucking begged me for them!

You practically dragged them away from me!

CARLA. That's not true –

LETTIE. Your shit's all broken and it made you crazy that I could have 'em and you couldn't.

You couldn't fucking stand it, so you took them away from me.

CARLA. They would be in some foster home if –

You have no idea.

You have no idea what we have done for you.

LETTIE. You haven't done shit for me.

You've done it all for yourself.

CARLA. Is this how you think?

Is this really how you think?

LETTIE. It doesn't have to be like, tomorrow.

But I'm gonna get a job and an apartment real soon and then –

CARLA. I can't believe this.

LETTIE. I know you wanted me to just stay gone.

CARLA. I have prayed night after night that you would get out and be okay.

That your children would know you.

LETTIE. Well, your prayers were answered, Carla.

CARLA. Not like this. It can't be like this.

CARLA.	**LETTIE.**
You can't just take them.	I'm a good mom. In my guts, I know that.

CARLA. You don't, Lettie.

LETTIE. I just never had a chance.

CARLA. You had plenty of chances. When will you / understand that?!

CARLA.	**LETTIE.**
Let's just take a minute / to figure it out.	I'm not saying tomorrow.

LETTIE. They're my kids.

Carla.

They're my kids.

CARLA. ...

LETTIE. Could you bring them over tomorrow? So I can talk to them about it?

Or I can come by your house?

CARLA. No.

LETTIE. Well then bring them here tomorrow after school and we can –

CARLA. I have the dinner shift tomorrow. I can't bring them –

LETTIE. Okay, well the day after. You got the dinner shift then?

CARLA. ...

LETTIE. Carla?

You got the dinner shift then?

CARLA. No.

LETTIE. Then bring them by?

CARLA. Can we wait till after – I want to have a nice Easter –

LETTIE. I'll take you to court.

And then I'll keep them away from you the way you've kept them away from me.

CARLA. How are you...

How did you get like this?

LETTIE. Got lucky in the genetic lottery, I guess.

I wanna talk to them in the next forty-eight hours, Carla. Okay?

LETTIE.	**CARLA**.
Okay?	Yes. Okay.

     (Quiet.)

LETTIE. Thank you. For everything.

CARLA. What?

LETTIE. Thank you. Really.

     *(**CARLA** looks at **LETTIE**. **CARLA** leaves.)*

Scene Thirteen

*(LETTIE outside Frank and Carla's house. She
knocks for a while. LAYLA answers the door.)*

LETTIE. Hey!

LAYLA. Hey. Happy Easter!

LETTIE. Oh. Yeah.

You too.

Carla and Frank here?

LAYLA. Yeah. I asked them to invite you over for Easter
dinner but they were all weird / about it. Sorry.

LETTIE. No, it's fine.

I, um. I been trying to call.

Did Carla talk to you?

LAYLA. About what?

FRANK. *(Offstage.)* Layla. Who is it?

(He enters. Sees LETTIE.)

What are you doing here?

LETTIE. I've been calling. You get my messages?

FRANK. ...

LETTIE. Carla was supposed to come to Spring House
yesterday. She told you that, yeah?

FRANK. Layla, go get your mother, please?

LAYLA. What's going on?

FRANK. Now, please.

LAYLA. Fine. Okay.

(She leaves.)

FRANK. I don't know what you think you're doing –

LETTIE. You can't keep them away from me, Frank.

FRANK. It is Easter / Sunday.

LETTIE. Big fucking deal. I been calling / and calling –

FRANK. You're not welcome in my house –

LETTIE. You can't / keep them from me.

FRANK. Lower your voice –

LETTIE. I'll take you to court.

Both of you.

You wanna do that?

(**CARLA** and **LAYLA** enter.)

CARLA. Lettie. What –

LETTIE. You were supposed to bring them by yesterday.

CARLA. I had to go to work, someone called in –

LETTIE. Then you ignore my calls. So I had to get on a bus – two buses – and come out here. You can't trap them here and –

LAYLA. Can someone please tell me / what's going on?

CARLA. Layla, sweetie, go upstairs –

LETTIE. Luisa, you can stay. You can do whatever you want.

CARLA. I don't want her to have –

LAYLA. Have to what?

LETTIE. I'm trying to be a part of your life and Carla and Frank here are having a real hard time with that.

CARLA. Please don't do this in front / of her.

LETTIE. She has a right to be a part of this conversation.

LAYLA. What conversation?

LETTIE. Do you want to spend time with me? Do you want to...have me in your life?

LAYLA. Yeah. Of course.

FRANK. That's not fair, Lettie.

LAYLA. What's not fair?

(**RIVER** comes down the stairs into the room.)

RIVER. What's going on?

LAYLA. I don't know. No one is making sense.

LETTIE. I want to spend time with you and Luisa, River. And Carla and Frank don't want that –

FRANK. No, she doesn't want to just spend time with you, she wants you to live with her.

Right? You want them to live with you?

(Beat.)

LETTIE. Not, like tomorrow, but –

FRANK. I don't understand why we're even having this conversation.

Let's cross that bridge when and if we come to –

LETTIE. It's time for us...

I want us to be a family.

LAYLA. Like...

How?

LETTIE. I found an apartment.

And. We can...

You guys will come and live with me.

RIVER. What?

LETTIE. In a couple of weeks.

CARLA.	**FRANK**.
Oh my god.	You really think you're gonna be able to take care of two teenagers?

LETTIE. Yeah. I do.

FRANK. You barely know them.

LETTIE. Neither do you!

FRANK. I don't know what you think the past seven years have been –

LETTIE. Shitty.

For all of us.

And I'm gonna do everything I can to make up for it.

FRANK. They have been in a house with two parents who love them and provide for them. Don't rip that away from them just because you're selfish.

LETTIE. I'm doing this for them.

FRANK. I find that hard to believe.

LETTIE. I don't care what you believe.

FRANK. You have the maturity level of a fifteen-year-old. When are you gonna grow up? Huh?

LETTIE. I am grown up, I'm trying to take care of my kids here, man.

FRANK. You gonna have them move into some rat trap apartment with you and then leave 'em there while you go out and get all fucked up?

CARLA. Frank, / stop.

LETTIE. Isn't Jesus gonna get mad at you for all this / cursing?

FRANK. You gonna steal River's record player and try to pawn it? You did it with his damn coin collection. Bet his record player is worth even more than those coins my father gave him for his sixth birthday. And then, after you sell all of their stuff you gonna start doing the other things you used to do for some quick cash?

LETTIE. Shut up. I'm telling you right now to –

FRANK. That's a great environment for two teenagers to be in.

Men – strangers – coming in and out at all –

Catching shit on / fire.

LETTIE. I'm gonna punch him, Carla. / Make him shut up or –

CARLA. Frank, stop. It is Easter / Sunday –

FRANK. You're gonna punch me?

LAYLA. Stop it!

CARLA. Enough. That's enough.

FRANK. There's no way I'm letting my kids –

RIVER. Yo, stop.

FRANK. – Be around someone like you. They're not gonna end up like you.

FRANK.	**LETTIE.**
And I'm gonna do whatever I can –	Well, they're sure as hell not gonna end up like you, you racist motherfucker.

RIVER. STOP.

(Beat.)

LETTIE. Sorry.

River, Luisa, I'm sorry. I just...

I'm just trying to work it out, you know.

FRANK. I can't do this.

I can't stand in here and do this.

LAYLA. Dad. It's okay.

LETTIE. We can start slow if you want.

We can hang out, have dinner.

Figure out when we can all move in / together.

FRANK. I can't believe this.

LAYLA. Dad, it's okay. We'll figure it out.

> (**FRANK** *walks out.*)

Right? This doesn't have to be a big deal?

LETTIE. Right. River? What do you think?

You guys come over?

We can all hang out some more and figure it out.

RIVER. ...

LETTIE. Yeah?

It'll be different. I promise.

Let me try, okay?

RIVER. ...

LETTIE. All right, then. Cool.

CARLA. Oh my.

LETTIE. Carla.

CARLA. Oh my goodness.

LAYLA. It's okay. This is fine.

(*To* **CARLA**.) Mom? Please? Let this be okay?

> (**CARLA** *looks at* **LAYLA** *and nods her head,*
> *"Okay."* **LAYLA** *hugs her.*)

It's fine. It really is.

Scene Fourteen

(**LETTIE**, **MINNY**, **LAYLA**, *and* **RIVER** *in the common room at Spring House.*)

MINNY. Then, he's like, "It says here that you were convicted of a felony." And I said, "Yeah. I was, a long time ago."

LETTIE. He can't legally ask you about that in an interview.

MINNY. I mean, not legally, but you know, you see the answer to that question on the application –

LAYLA. I would wanna ask.

MINNY. So he asks and I'm like, "Shit. Here we go again." I've been on at least forty interviews since I got out of the program and I'm just tired of this shit, you know? Then, he's like, "Um... I know I'm not supposed to –

LETTIE. See?

MINNY. – But, can I ask, what you were convicted of?"

LETTIE. At least he didn't ask, "What did you do?"

MINNY. I'm quiet for a second and I'm so sick of this shit. I'm like, "Fuck it." So I say, "Murder." And he doesn't say nothing.

LETTIE. Oh shit.

MINNY. And then I go, "I didn't get this job that I really wanted. So, I found the guy that interviewed me, shot him, cut his dick off and then stuffed it in his mouth. Comanche style. Craziest thing I ever did, man."

LETTIE. Minny!

LAYLA. Did you really say that?

MINNY. I thought it was funny!

LETTIE. What did the guy do?

MINNY. He stared at me like, "What the fuck?" And then I smiled, like, "I'm just kidding, man."

LAYLA. Oh my god.

MINNY. And he gave like a nervous laugh and tried to keep going with the interview.

But I start freaking out, like, "Why did I just do that?"

LETTIE. Yeah, you can't be doing that!

MINNY. I know, but I thought it was funny!

LETTIE. So, you got the job, right?

(They all laugh.)

LAYLA. What did you want to do, Minny?

MINNY. Hmmm?

LAYLA. Before you...

Like, what did you want to be?

(Beat.)

MINNY. Hm. I don't know. A mom. I guess.

LAYLA. I want to be an actress.

MINNY. Oh yeah?

LAYLA. Yep.

MINNY. Okay. Well that's good. Hollywood needs someone besides J.Lo to play the maid. One day she might look old and the movies like their Latina maids young and spicy.

LETTIE. Minny!

MINNY. What? It's true! You can make a career out of it – Hollywood maid is a good gig!

LETTIE. Don't listen to her.

*(The mood is still light, but **LAYLA** stays quiet.)*

MINNY. What about you, River?

RIVER. ...

LETTIE. Music. He wants to be a producer.

MINNY. It's good you two have chosen practical professions.

RIVER. You can go after some job because you think it's like a sure thing and you get fucked anyway.

I mean, look at Frank.

LAYLA. River.

LETTIE. What's going on with Frank?

RIVER. He lost his job like two months ago. But just now told us.

LAYLA. The factory shut down.

RIVER. Like, six hundred people are fucked.

So. Might as well go after something you actually like.

MINNY. Yeah, like your mom did with welding.

LETTIE. Shut up.

MINNY. She didn't make it even halfway through that program.

LAYLA. You...you're not doing the program anymore?

LETTIE. Yeah. No.

MINNY. She was a safety hazard.

People wanted to start doing fire drills because of her.

(Beat.)

RIVER. You got kicked out?

LETTIE. It wasn't a good fit.

RIVER. *(To MINNY.)* Do you live here, too?

MINNY. Yeah. For now. Your mom helped me out. Got me a spot here.

But once I have a job I'll be able to get something.

RIVER. *(To LETTIE.)* But you don't have a job and you were able to get something? Right?

You found an apartment?

Or, am I like, confused –

LETTIE. No, no. I found something.

(She pulls a pamphlet out and hands it to **RIVER.***)*

Here.

RIVER. This isn't near our school.

LETTIE. Yeah. I tried, but –

RIVER. How are you gonna pay for this?

LETTIE. I'm gonna get a job.

RIVER. But you just got fired –

LETTIE. I didn't get –

RIVER. Just, how are you able to afford one of these apartments?

RIVER.   LETTIE.
    I mean, it's low-income   I'll be able –
    housing, clearly, but how
    will you –

LETTIE. It'll be fine. I got it.

LAYLA. We can decorate it?

LETTIE. Whatever you want.

LAYLA. Can I paint my room? Like, whatever color I want
    it –

RIVER. You're not gonna have a room.

        (Beat.)

LAYLA. Oh. I just...

LETTIE. One day you will. Just not –

RIVER. How is she ever gonna have a room? I mean, you
    can't even afford to order pizza. This is like frozen pizza
    from the Jewel.

LETTIE. Hey, man fucking chill.

RIVER. What?

LETTIE. Stop being shitty.

LAYLA. You don't have to talk like –

LETTIE. Sorry.
    I'm sorry.
    I shouldn't have... Sorry.
    ...
    How are rehearsals going? For the play?

LAYLA. Fine.

MINNY. What play?

LETTIE. *Annie.*
    She beat out like a ton of girls for Pepper.

MINNY. Which one is Pepper?

LETTIE. That orphan that's the asshole.

LAYLA. She's misunderstood.
    She's not...

LETTIE. You thought it was funny when I called her that before.

I was joking.

LAYLA. Yeah, but...

It's like, my part.

LETTIE. Oh, I didn't mean...

Sorry. I was joking.

(Beat.)

LAYLA. It's already eight.

LETTIE. Oh, yeah. Shit. Okay.

LAYLA. We should get to the bus.

LETTIE. Yeah. Yeah. Okay.

MINNY. You're going with them?

RIVER. We're fine.

LETTIE. No, no. I'm coming.

MINNY. You're not gonna get back until after eleven.

LETTIE. Shit.

LAYLA. What?

LETTIE. We have – uh, like, a curfew.

LAYLA. Oh.

RIVER. We can go by ourselves –

LETTIE. No. No.

I'll explain it to them tomorrow. It'll be fine.

Come on. Let's go.

Scene Fifteen

(LETTIE, RIVER, and LAYLA wait at the bus stop.)

LETTIE. Shit. It shoulda been here twenty minutes ago.

LAYLA. It's freezing.

LETTIE. I know. I'm sorry.

LAYLA. Are you gonna get a car?

LETTIE. Yeah.

RIVER. The car and the apartment and the job, yeah?

LAYLA. I can't wait to get a car.

   Two years and I'll be able to drive.

RIVER. Get used to the bus.

LAYLA. What?

RIVER. You're not gonna get a car, you're not gonna get your own room –

LETTIE. River.

RIVER. What?

LETTIE. ...

   You wanna do some stuff from your play?

   Like, sing a song from it or something?

LAYLA. Not really.

LETTIE. It'll make the time go faster.

   We can practice your lines or whatever.

   Come on. It'll be fun.

LAYLA. Fine.

      *(She digs through her backpack, looking for
      her script.)*

LETTIE. Okay. Cool.

      *(LAYLA finds the script, flips to a page, and
      hands it to LETTIE.)*

LAYLA. Start here.

LETTIE. Okay.

LAYLA. Read Annie's lines.

LETTIE. Okay.

Um.

> *(She reads.)*

So, this Molly girl just wet the bed? How old is she supposed –

LAYLA. It doesn't matter, it's just…

Like, she's the baby of the orphanage and it's this whole thing.

LETTIE. That's fucked.

LAYLA. Just start.

(Pointing.) Here, with that line.

LETTIE. Okay, um…

> *(She looks at the script, then tries to be Annie.)*

"It's okay, it was –"

> (**RIVER** *has taken out a one-hitter and lights up. He takes a drag.)*

Yo, what are you doing?

RIVER. What?

LETTIE. Are you fucking kidding me right now?

LAYLA. River! Are you smoking weed right now?

LETTIE. You gotta be fucking / kidding me –

RIVER. It's not a big deal. It's weed.

LETTIE. Put that shit away.

> (**RIVER** *takes another drag.)*

I said put it away.

RIVER. Yeah, yeah.

LETTIE. You know that if –

I could get in big trouble, I could get arrested if I'm even anywhere near that shit.

RIVER. That's not my problem.

LAYLA. River.

RIVER. What? That's her problem, not mine.

LETTIE. Man, you're acting like a little punk.

RIVER. What? Oh, I'm sorry. You want some?

LETTIE. Shut the fuck up, man.

RIVER. You're gonna tell me to shut the fuck up?
Seriously?

LETTIE. Is that all you ever say?
"Seriously?"

RIVER. Okay.

LETTIE. Hey, put that away.

> *(She tries to take the one-hitter out of **RIVER**'s
> hand. He jerks it away. She reaches and grabs
> his wrist, hard.)*

RIVER. Don't touch me.

LETTIE. I told you to put that away.

RIVER. Let go of me.

LAYLA. River, just put it –

> *(She is still holding his arm, trying to wrestle
> the pot away.)*

LETTIE. Give it to me.
Give it to me right now.

RIVER. You gonna hit me? That what you're gonna do? Hit
me?

LETTIE. Easy, man.

RIVER. That what you're gonna do right now?

> *(Quiet. **LETTIE** lets go of his hand.)*

Yeah.

LETTIE. Just put it away.

RIVER. I remember that shit.

RIVER.	**LETTIE.**
I remember all of it.	Okay.

RIVER. Layla might not remember –

LAYLA. Remember what –

RIVER. But I do.
I know who you are.

LETTIE. Okay, just chill. Chill.

RIVER. You wanna fucking come back here and act like we're gonna be some family?

LETTIE. All right.

RIVER. You gonna get frozen pizza and have us over in your fucking halfway house with your girlfriend and everything is cool? That this is all cool?

LETTIE. I'm just trying –

RIVER. I don't care. I don't care what you're trying. I really don't.

LAYLA. River.

RIVER. Nah. you know what? Fuck it.

(He starts walking away. LETTIE grabs him.)

LETTIE. Hey. You can't just –

RIVER. I told you not to touch me.

(He shoves LETTIE off. He starts walking away again.)

LAYLA. River, stop it! Stop.

LETTIE. Don't shove me, man.

(She grabs RIVER again. This time he shoves her really hard.)

Hey.

(RIVER shoves her again.)

LAYLA. River, stop.

LETTIE. Don't fucking shove me again.

RIVER. Or what. Huh? Or what?

(He shoves LETTIE again. She instantly slaps him in the face.)

(Beat.)

Yeah. There you are. Good to see you again.

LETTIE. Hey.

Hey. I'm sorry but –

I'm sorry –

(She tries to grab **RIVER,** *to hold him. He shoves her away and takes off.)*

LETTIE. Hey!

LAYLA. River!

LETTIE. River! Stop.

LAYLA. Stop!

Scene Sixteen

(**LETTIE**, **LAYLA**, *and* **CARLA** *all sit in the kitchen.*
FRANK *is on the phone.*)

FRANK. Right?

But you have to at least –

He's seventeen.

Okay.

Yes.

Thank you.

CARLA. What'd they say?

FRANK. They have two squad cars looking for him.

They can't file anything yet since it's only been a few hours.

CARLA. It's been eight hours. Not a few. Eight.

FRANK. They can't file anything until twenty-four hours after someone has gone missing.

LAYLA. Ian's uncle is a cop. I can ask –

FRANK. There are two cars out. They'll find him.

LETTIE. I...uh...

Minny is out looking in the neighborhood. She told the folks at the house and they're gonna be looking out. So.

LAYLA. I feel like we looked everywhere around there.

LETTIE. Yeah. But maybe once it gets light...you know?

LAYLA. Yeah.

FRANK. He's okay. It's gonna be okay.

He'll come home and it will be fine.

(*Quiet.*)

LETTIE. I shouldn't have...

I shouldn't have lost my temper like that.

I shouldn't have touched him.

LAYLA. He lost his temper, too.

CARLA. But he's the child.

(*Beat.*)

LETTIE. What?

CARLA. He gets to lose his temper.

He's the child.

He gets to behave badly.

You don't.

LETTIE. Okay, Carla.

LAYLA. *(To* **LETTIE**.*)* He was acting like a jerk. It's not your fault.

CARLA. It is her fault.

If something happens to him...

It's her fault.

FRANK. Carla.

CARLA. No. I'm done.

(To **LETTIE**.*)* You messed up.

And you're gonna do it again and again and again.

And these children are always gonna be the ones who suffer.

This is what you do.

"I'm gonna do right. I'm gonna get it together and do right."

Remember? You said that the first time you got out.

You swore up and down that that was it.

Then, you met that monster and moved down to Texas and forgot you had a baby boy at home and just did whatever the hell he wanted you to. You do his drugs and sell his drugs and have his baby and then call me crying, telling me that you had to get out of there. That you were ready to make a change and you even swore that you wanted Jesus in your life. That you were ready. And I said, "Okay, Lettie. Bring your baby girl, come on back, you can move in with us." Then right back at it. Doing things that make me sick to my stomach.

You almost killed your own child.

But you didn't give a damn. Just, back to Texas, back to the man –

LETTIE. You kicked me out.

CARLA. No, after you almost burned down our entire house, I told you you could stay if you got sober. But you made your choice and back to Texas, back to all of it. Then you're stupid enough to agree to carry it across state lines? You're stupid and you don't give a damn. It's whatever you want, just like our mom. Just do whatever the hell you want because somebody will come along and clean up the mess. I'm so tired of it. You make me curse and you make me mean and you make me tired. And you're gonna make them tired like you've made me.

LETTIE. I was a child too.

You know?

I was a child when all that happened.

CARLA. I don't care. I don't care.

LETTIE. So, River can behave badly because he's a child but I couldn't?

Give me a break.

CARLA. Lettie, you had a baby. You don't get to –

LETTIE. You have no idea what I lived through.

FRANK. Layla, let's go up –

LETTIE. No, let her stay.

I want her to know that I wasn't just some fuck-up.

That I was trying to get by however I could growing up with junkie parents.

You wanna cry and bitch about how Mom left you, Carla? You're lucky!

You're lucky you didn't have to pick her up off the floor, you're lucky you didn't have to watch her eyes roll in the back of her head, you're lucky one of her friends didn't get you pregnant when you were fifteen.

You wanna talk about how I had everything?

How I had everything and you had nothing?

That's garbage. That's a fucking lie.

I wish I had the nothing that you had.

FRANK. Come on, Layla. Let's get you upstairs –

LETTIE. I never had a goddamn chance.

FRANK. Please don't take the Lord's / name in –

LETTIE. I never had a chance to be a kid and I never had a chance to be an adult.

CARLA. That was your choice. You're the one who did the drugs, you're the –

LETTIE. It's all I could fucking do to get through the goddamn day! And now, I'm not doing that shit and trust me it's hard to get through ever since I've been out, but I've done it. That's who I am, I'm standing here telling you that's who I am!

LAYLA. Lettie, please. Please stop.

FRANK.	**LETTIE.**
Shh. It's gonna / be okay.	I'm your mom! Please, please don't call –

FRANK. Come on, Layla.

LETTIE. I'm her mom, Frank!

> *(Just then, the door opens and **RIVER** walks in.)*

CARLA. Oh thank god.

> *(She rushes to him and puts her arms around him. **LAYLA** runs to him and wraps her arms around him and **CARLA**. **FRANK**, relieved to the point of tears, walks to them and wraps his arms around them all. **LETTIE** watches as they hold one another. From the hug, we can hear **RIVER**.)*

RIVER. I'm sorry.

CARLA. It's okay.

RIVER. I just walked around. All over. I just needed some space.

FRANK. It's okay. We love you so much. You know that, right? You know how much we love you?

RIVER. I do. Yeah.

Scene Seventeen

(**LETTIE** *walks into the common room at Spring House.* **MINNY** *is up, waiting.*)

MINNY. Did they find him?

LETTIE. He came back to the house.

He was out just walking around.

Needed some space.

MINNY. Oh, thank god. Right?

Jesus I was worried.

LETTIE. Me too.

(*Quiet.*)

MINNY. Everything okay?

Is he okay?

LETTIE. Yeah. Yeah.

MINNY. Is Luisa?

LETTIE. Yeah.

MINNY. You want some coffee?

(**LETTIE** *nods and* **MINNY** *goes to the kitchen.* **LETTIE** *is alone.*)

(**MINNY** *comes back in with the coffee.*)

Your sister pissed?

LETTIE. None of it was good, you know?

I lost my temper.

MINNY. It's okay.

LETTIE. I got so mad. I got so fucking mad.

MINNY. You're allowed to get mad.

LETTIE. No. I'm not.

You talk to them? About me being gone?

MINNY. Yeah. They told me to tell you to go down and see them when you got back.

LETTIE. Shit.

MINNY. Maybe just a warning or something?

LETTIE. What a fucking joke.

MINNY. What?

LETTIE. All this.

I'm always gonna fuck up.

MINNY. That's not true.

You're not. Hey?

You're not.

LETTIE. You think...

Like, is this shit really gonna work out?

MINNY. You found that apartment, I'm going on interviews –

LETTIE. They're never gonna give me that apartment.

That's never gonna happen.

Not really.

MINNY. Yes, it will.

LETTIE. We're gonna get jobs and we're gonna go to work and we're gonna be fine and we're gonna have money and we're gonna have a house and we're gonna be real people?

You think that's really gonna happen?

MINNY. ...

LETTIE. Like, if we're being realistic?

MINNY. Come on, Lettie.

LETTIE. You said I had to start being realistic. So.

I'm trying here.

You think any of that is gonna happen?

(*Quiet.*)

MINNY. I don't know.

(*Quiet.*)

LETTIE. My mom was a fuck-up. It was bad, you know?

So I started getting high. With her, without her, whatever.

I was just a kid but it had already gotten me.

I tried and tried but couldn't get away from it.

Then, when I was in, I became thankful. It took some time, but I became so thankful that I had a chance to

just exist for a minute. And, Minny, I know it sounds
stupid, but when I was in there, I was able to convince
myself...

MINNY. What?

LETTIE. I was able to convince myself that I wasn't a loser.
That I had something to give.
That I could be a good mom.

MINNY. You do, you are –

LETTIE. No. It's always gonna come back for me.
And I'll lose. Every time I will.
I can't get away from it, can I?

MINNY. Get away from what?

LETTIE. ...

> *(Quiet.)*

MINNY. You know how they always tell us, "You have to
forgive yourself. You have to move forward.
Take what you've learned and move forward."
I'll never be able to really do that.

LETTIE. Yeah.

MINNY. I don't think there's really any moving forward.
I think there's just moving along.

LETTIE. ...

MINNY. I know you love them.
And I know what you're really like.
I think I do, at least.
...
So.
What are you gonna do?

Scene Eighteen

(*Eight months later.* **LETTIE**, **CARLA**, **FRANK**, **LAYLA**, *and* **RIVER** *at the dinner table. It's a different dinner table, in a different house, in a different town.*)

(**CARLA** *blesses the food.*)

CARLA. Dear Heavenly Father,

This Thanksgiving we pause to reflect on the many blessings bestowed upon us throughout the year.

…

Thank you for these gifts, which we are about to receive.

Thank you for family.

Thank you for letting us sit here, together, on this day, at this table.

Bless this food to our use, and us to thy service. Fill our hearts with grateful praise.

Amen.

ALL. Amen.

(*They pass around food in styrofoam containers but eat off glass plates.*)

FRANK. How was the trip?

LETTIE. Fine.

FRANK. What, four hours?

LETTIE. About, yeah.

FRANK. And there's a bus?

LETTIE. A Greyhound.

Easy.

FRANK. And it's fine, with your parole –

LETTIE. Yeah. Filled out all the forms, got a pass.

FRANK. Great. And you'll be able to get a bus back after dinner?

LETTIE. Yeah. There's not a direct one that late, but I'll transfer. No problem.

FRANK. That's great.

LETTIE. *(Re: the food.)* This is good.

Thank you.

CARLA. I know I should cook for Thanksgiving but I just couldn't get it / together this year.

FRANK. I told her not to worry about it. We've been busy and –

CARLA. I know, I know. But it's Thanksgiving –

FRANK. Honey, this food is great. I think it's great we don't have –

CARLA. It's good, right? The food? I do feel like all of this is very good.

LETTIE. Yeah, it really is.

CARLA. I like this Jewel much better than my old one.

The food is fresher, I think.

FRANK. I think so too.

LETTIE. Yeah, all of this tastes great.

And this house, it's really nice.

CARLA. Thank you.

We like it.

LETTIE. And Frank your job?

When I talked to Carla, she said that you really liked it.

FRANK. It's still new and I'm the oldest guy on the floor. But yeah, I'm getting used to it.

LETTIE. Cool.

FRANK. Just glad I could find something.

Of course, I wish we didn't have to move. But.

What can you do?

LETTIE. Yeah, no. It's great that you found something.

CARLA. It is. We are very blessed.

And we are so happy that you were able to finally get out here.

LETTIE. Yeah, me too. Just been hard to figure out when I could make the trip, money, all that.

School is good?

Layla? You like school?

LAYLA. Sure.

LETTIE. You doing your acting and all your stuff?

LAYLA. Not really.

LETTIE. No?

CARLA. She's doing some stuff...

I told you about how she's doing Junior ROTC.

LETTIE. Yeah, ROTC. That's like Army / stuff, yeah?

CARLA. Scholarships. ROTC is great for scholarships.

LETTIE. Right.

Well, with that and your grades it should be no problem, huh?

LAYLA. My grades aren't great.

CARLA. They're fine, honey.

FRANK. It's been an adjustment for all of us.

LETTIE. Oh. Yeah, of course.

CARLA. She'll get them back up.

She will, I know she will.

LAYLA. Whatever.

LETTIE. Yeah, you're super smart, you'll figure it out.

LAYLA. Seriously, it's fine.

(*Quiet.*)

LETTIE. (*To* **RIVER.**) And you?

RIVER. What?

LETTIE. You good?

RIVER. Sure. Yeah.

LETTIE. Congratulations on your graduation.

I tried to get out here, but I had just started the job and they wouldn't budge with my schedule. Carla sent me a picture, though.

You looked great in your cap and gown.

CARLA. Didn't he?

LETTIE. You get the gift I sent –

RIVER. Yeah.

LETTIE. Carla said you're taking the year off before college, right?

RIVER. Yeah.

LETTIE. Doing your music?

CARLA. We have a basement. River has all his music stuff down there.

His records, record player, speakers.

LETTIE. That's awesome.

CARLA. Frank set it up real neat down there.

LETTIE. Oh yeah?

CARLA. River can show you after dinner.

FRANK. It's not much, but it's like his own little studio or something.

LETTIE. Oh, wow.

FRANK. Yeah, and River actually just started as an apprentice at my factory.

They gave him free training, then put him right into the apprenticeship.

LETTIE. That's...

Cool. That's great.

FRANK. It is.

LETTIE. Are you...

Do you like it, River?

RIVER. Yeah.

I do.

FRANK. He's doing great.

LETTIE. Awesome.

FRANK. Lettie, Carla said you found a job.

LETTIE. Yeah.

FRANK. Cleaning, right, for –

LETTIE. Yeah. For Truman College.

CARLA. Oh, I hear Truman is a wonderful community college.

LETTIE. Yeah, I don't know.

I just clean it.

CARLA. No, I know, I just heard –

Sorry, I didn't mean –

LETTIE. It's all good, Carlz. Really.

FRANK. And the trades, you never got to finish that /
program?

LETTIE. No.

FRANK. Well, at least you're doing something. You know, for
work.

LETTIE. Yeah.

FRANK. You're still at Spring House?

LETTIE. Nah...

All that curfew stuff. Wasn't a good fit.

I'm at a different place now. It's fine.

Minny's still at Spring House, though.

CARLA. Are you still searching – looking for an apartment?

LETTIE. Yeah. Yeah. A few places have just, you know...

Fallen through.

And there are long waiting lists.

But I'll get something soon.

CARLA. Well, that's great.

FRANK. I'm proud of you, Lettie.

LETTIE. Huh?

FRANK. You're working hard, trying to lead an honest life.

That's not easy.

LETTIE. *(Trying to joke.)* Yeah. Being a sober janitor is pretty
darn tough.

...

Whatever it takes to come out here and have dinner.

To see you guys.

FRANK. Good. That's good.

CARLA. It sure is.

I like this IHOP better too, actually.

I have mostly breakfast shifts and weekends. And the
customers are much more polite.

I think it's true: the people in Wisconsin are nicer.

LETTIE. Awesome.

CARLA. Lettie, you're welcome to join us for Christmas. If you can find a way out here we would love to have you.

LETTIE. Thanks. I'll try and survive until then.

FRANK. You make sure and do that, all right?

LETTIE. Yeah. Yeah. I will.

Thanks, Carlz. That sounds great.

CARLA. Of course.

FRANK. I gotta say...

CARLA. What?

FRANK. This is real nice.

LETTIE. It is.

End of Play

9 780573 708695